MW00889756

The Voice of the Good Shepherd

A Collection of Short Stories

by Susan Perry

illustrated by Caryn Baker

authorHOUSE®

AuthorHouse™
1663 Liberty Drive
Bloomington, IN 47403
www.authorhouse.com
Phone: 1 (800) 839-8640

Published by AuthorHouse 03/05/2020

ISBN: 978-1-7283-4521-5 (sc)
ISBN: 978-1-7283-4519-2 (hc)
ISBN: 978-1-7283-4520-8 (e)

Library of Congress Control Number: 2020901890

Print information available on the last page.

This is dedicated to Reggie, our four children and five grandchildren.

A special thanks to Caryn, Isabella, and Becky for the encouragement and support that made this possible.

Table of Contents

I am the good shepherd. The good shepherd sacrifices his life for his sheep.

—John 10:11

Part One

I praise you because I am fearfully and wonderfully made: Your works are wonderful, I know that full well.
—Psalms 139:14

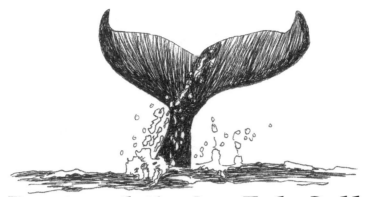

Jonah and the Big Fish, Betty

The waters of the Mediterranean were warm and relaxing to Betty. She loved to swim and play in the large open sea. Her favorite game was "sing and spring," as she called it. She would spring high into the air, twirling her large body while singing at the top of her voice, sending a great splash as she fell back into the water.

Betty was a very large fish, much larger than the other fish in her school. She was often made fun of. School became her least favorite place to be, and she spent much of her time alone.

Betty couldn't understand why the other fish disliked her because of her size. *If only they would give me a chance,* she thought.

Betty had finished a long day at school and was heading home when she heard a cry for help. She looked around to see a scared skinny seagull flapping his wings in an attempt to escape the mouth of a large shark. Betty sprang into action, ramming the shark as hard as she could. The old shark quickly took off. Betty watched to make sure he didn't return.

"Thank you for saving me," said the seagull. "I usually don't come this far from the shore, but I was daydreaming again and lost track of my location.

"My name is Jack. I am very grateful you came along when you did," Jack added. "Most of the other fish would not have cared if that old shark ate me or not."

"It's nice to meet you," said Betty. "My name is Betty. I come this way on my way home from school. You really need to be careful coming out this far. There are always sharks hanging around out here."

Betty and Jack formed an immediate friendship. They had a lot in common for a big fish and a skinny seagull.

Betty and Jack met after school most days. They shared how they were both mistreated for looking different and vowed to never treat anyone the way they were treated.

Betty had a good home, with a loving mom and dad. Her parents tried to reassure her that she was created large for a reason. "Betty, you are created exactly the way God wanted you to be. Many fish don't have the loving heart you have. I am proud of the fish you are," said her mom.

Betty couldn't help but wish she looked like the other fish at school. She would often lie on the big seaweed sofa and daydream of being a beautiful fish, with the grace of a swan.

It was getting late as Betty headed to her room to get ready for bed. Her parents always came in to pray and give her a good night kiss. Even though Betty felt too old for the kiss, it still made her feel loved.

Betty had just pulled the covers up when she heard a soft voice saying her name. She looked around, thinking Jack had come by. *Maybe I was dreaming, but I'm still awake,* thought Betty. She pulled the covers up close to her face, hoping to go to sleep.

"Betty," said the voice.

Slowly she peeked out from under the covers. "Y-yes," she answered.

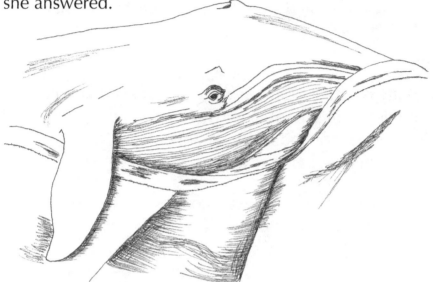

"Don't be afraid, Betty. God has sent me to ask for your help," said the angel.

"Too late, Mr. Angel. I'm already terrified. You're the first angel I've ever seen," replied Betty, adding, "Why would God want my help? I'm just a kid."

"God has a mission that will require a large fish, and he wants you for the job," said the angel.

"Well, I'm your girl. I'm the biggest fish in the sea. Just ask any of the other fish at my school," Betty laughed. "Do you have a name? I mean does God name His angels? Oh, wow. That was rude. Sorry, Mr. Angel. I'm really nervous," stuttered Betty.

"It's okay, Betty. I understand. It's not every day that God sends an angel asking for your help. My name is Gabriel. I'm God's messenger angel," answered Gabriel.

"Mr. Gabriel, what if I don't want to do this mission?" asked Betty.

"Betty, God gives us all the right to choose. It will be your choice whether to accept God's call or not," replied Gabriel.

"Well, since you put it like that, I'll go. But do you think that my friend Jack could come with me?" asked Betty.

"Of course, if Jack wants to come. I'm sure God could use him," said Gabriel, adding, "I will meet you and Jack after school in your usual meeting place."

"You know where we always meet?" asked Betty.

"Remember, God sees and knows everything, Betty." Gabriel smiled.

Suddenly, the angel was gone, and her bedroom seemed quieter than ever before. Betty lay back in her soft bed, wondering what God could possibly want from her.

Sleep eventually won over her vivid imagination.

The bright light of day woke Betty early the next morning. She jumped out of bed, rushing to get ready for school. She wanted to leave early and find Jack. She could hardly wait to tell him about their mission.

"No time for breakfast, Mom. I have to hurry," said Betty.

"Betty, you never turn down food. Are you sick, dear?" asked mom.

"Nope. I just have a mission to do. I mean a project," shouted Betty.

After a little searching, she found Jack catching fish with his beak from the old port pier.

"Jack," shouted Betty.

"Good morning, Betty," answered Jack.

"Jack, come out here. I have great news for you."

"What's going on, Betty? You never come here in the mornings," said Jack.

"Jack, you're not going to believe who I talked to last night," said Betty.

"Who? Just tell me. I'll never guess," answered Jack.

"It was an angel named Gabriel. God sent him to ask for my help. Oh, and he said He could also use you. What do you think? Will you go with me?" asked Betty.

"Well, what is the mission?" asked Jack.

"I-I don't know," answered Betty.

"Okay. When do we go?" asked Jack.

"I-I don't know," answered Betty.

"Do you know anything about this mission?" asked Jack.

"Not really. But it will be an adventure, Jack. Come on. Go with me," cried Betty.

"Not until I have more information," said Jack.

"I'm meeting Mr. Gabriel today after school in our usual meeting place. Be there, and he will tell us more about God's plan. See you this afternoon," shouted Betty.

Betty thought the day would never end as she watched the clock. Finally, the last bell of the day sounded, and Betty was off as fast as she could swim.

There on a floating log sat Jack. It was a relief to see her friend waiting for her.

"Hi, Jack," shouted Betty.

"Hi, Betty. Where's this angel you were telling me about?" asked Jack.

"I'm sure he will be here soon," said Betty.

"Betty, are you sure this was not one of your crazy dreams?" asked Jack.

"No, Jack, it's not a dream," answered Gabriel.

"Y-you a-are r-real," stuttered Jack.

"Yes, Jack, I'm real. And I'm glad you are both here. We have a lot to discuss, so let's gets started," said Gabriel.

"There is a human by the name of Jonah. He will travel to the port of Joppa. Jonah is a good man who loves God very much. God has given him a mission that scares him and has caused him to try and run from God.

"God told Jonah to go to the wicked city of Nineveh and tell the people of His love for them. Jonah was afraid to go to such a wicked place. He decided to board a ship in Joppa that was headed for Tarshish, which is in the opposite direction of … Nineveh," Gabriel explained.

"I know all about Nineveh, and I don't blame Jonah. There are some bad people in that city," added Jack.

"You're right, but God promised to protect Jonah. The people of Nineveh also deserve to know about God's love," said Gabriel. "God has a plan to get Jonah back on the right track. That's where you two come in.

"Listen closely. This is God's plan. Betty, because of your size and strength, you can swim through a rough storm. You are also large enough to swallow and carry a large load," Gabriel began.

"I can sure do that, I once swallowed this big old squid in one bite. Jack says I could swallow a whole ship." Betty laughed uncomfortably. "Oh no. Am I going to have to swallow that ship?" she cried.

"No, Betty. God will bring a great storm. The ship will be tossed and turned in the rough waters. The crew will become afraid and call on their gods, but there will be no answer. Captain Royce will go below to wake Jonah and tell him to call on his God. Jonah will see what's happening and will realize that God is showing him that he cannot run or hide from Him. Jonah will know that the only way to save the ship and its crew is to be thrown overboard.

"Betty, you will be there to swallow Jonah," instructed Gabriel.

"No way. I can't stand the smell of humans, much less swallow one," cried Betty.

"Betty, God will take away the smell and taste of Jonah. You will just gently carry him in your belly for three days. You will need to eat lots of seaweed so it will be soft and comfortable for him," said Gabriel.

"Mr. Gabriel, I don't understand God's plan at all. How is this going to help Jonah?" asked Betty.

"Some things can't be explained, Betty. God has a perfect plan, and we just have to trust Him," said Gabriel.

"Well, it's time for me to go, Betty and Jack," the angel added. "God will be with you. Start watching for dark clouds. It's almost time."

Jack pointed Betty to some seaweed. "Eat as much as you can, Betty. It needs to be warm and cozy in your belly," said jack.

"Jack, look. I see dark clouds rolling in from the south. The storm will be here soon. Hurry and go locate the ship," said Betty.

Jack flew off in the direction of Tarshish looking closely for any sign of the ship. Suddenly, he saw it—a large ship headed directly toward Tarshish.

There it is. That has to be the right ship, thought Jack.

He flew closer and looked for something that would confirm it was the ship Jonah was on.

"Jonah, you must go below. The weather is making a change, and you'll be safer there," said Captain Royce.

Hearing Captain Royce talking to Jonah, Jack knew it was the right ship. *Now to direct Betty to it,* he thought.

Jack flew with all his might in the strong winds. He had to hurry and get Betty before he lost the location of the ship.

"Betty, I found it. Follow me. It's not far, but the storm is getting worse. So we'll need to hurry," shouted Jack.

"I'm right behind you," responded Betty.

"There it is. Good luck," said Jack.

Betty smiled at her friend. She felt special for the first time in her life. She stopped and thanked God for her friend and the opportunity to help with such an important mission.

Betty slowly moved toward the ship, fighting the strong winds and waters. As she got closer to the large ship, she could hear the crew screaming for help from their gods. She then heard the voice of the captain calling for Jonah to come up and pray to his God. Betty couldn't believe it was happening just as the angel had said it would.

"Captain, the storm is my fault. I have disobeyed my God, and He has brought this storm on us. Please, you must throw me overboard. That is the only way God will calm the storm," cried Jonah.

"Are you sure, Jonah? I don't understand your God," said Captain Royce.

"It will be okay. He will protect me. Please just have your men throw me over," said Jonah.

"Silas, John, throw him over as he says," ordered the captain.

This is it, thought Betty.

The two men lifted Jonah and threw him over the rails into the raging waters. Before Jonah hit the water, the winds were calm, and the water became still. Betty heard the captain declare that Jonah's God was the true God, and that was who they would worship.

As Jonah sunk in the deep water, Betty quickly opened her large mouth and swallowed him up. She heard Jonah cry out to God for forgiveness. It then became very quiet, except for the sweet whispers of God speaking to Jonah.

Betty slowly swam the beautiful waters while she housed Jonah. On the third day, as instructed, Betty came in close to the shore of Nineveh.

"Spit him out, Betty," said God.

Betty spit Jonah onto the shores of Nineveh, where she heard him immediately begin to tell the people of this wicked city God's message to them.

Betty turned and started home. She felt different. She knew that God did have a plan, not just for her but also for everyone. She would never see herself again as anything other than a fearfully and wonderfully made creation of the one true God.

Betty would go back to school, forgive the mean words of her peers, and always do her best to share God's message.

God would call on Betty and Jack many other times in their lives, and each time they would give their best for Him. Betty would later become loved and respected by all the fish who came to know her.

Max & Millie,
Two Monkeys on the Ark

In the Middle Eastern part of the world, there lived a man named Noah. He was a good and righteous man who found favor with God. Noah loved and obeyed God.

Now God saw that all the earth had become very bad. It was full of evil, and God decided to start over. He decided to clean the earth with a flood.

One day as Noah was working in the fields, God spoke to him. "Noah, I have decided to clean the world with a great flood. I want you to build a large boat from cypress wood and waterproof it inside and out with tar. Make it 450 feet long, 75 feet wide, and 45 feet high. Leave an eighteen-inch opening from the roof all the way around the boat. Put the door on the side, and build three decks inside the boat—a lower, middle, and upper deck."

Noah quickly called his family together to tell them about the strange instructions God had given him about building a boat. He told them that he did not understand what a boat was or even a flood, but he loved God and planned to obey Him.

"Papa, this is crazy," shouted his son Ham.

"I agree," cried another son, Shem.

"Well, Japheth, I haven't heard from you. What is your opinion, my son?" asked Noah.

"Papa, I don't always understand what God is doing, but he is good to us and would never tell us to do the wrong thing," said Japheth.

"Japheth is right. We will follow God's instructions to the letter," said Noah.

"Now that we have agreed to build the boat, God also wants us to gather a pair of all animals, one male and one female of every kind. We're also to gather pairs of all the birds and of every small creature that crawls along the ground. We are to stock the boat with enough food for all the animals and for our family."

"Papa, you have to be kidding. How will we do that?" asked Ham.

"Ham, you worry too much. God will show us. First, we build the boat, and then God will take care of the rest," said Noah.

Noah and his wife walked down by the small creek that ran along their property. Lydia, Noah's wife, was a good and kind woman who also loved God. She gave Noah her blessing and pledged to do all she could to help.

Early the next morning, Noah and his three sons, Shem, Ham, and Japheth, began the project God had given them to do. When they roped off the place where they were to build the boat, Noah and his sons knelt and gave thanks to God for all they had. They asked for His blessing on this large boat they would build.

The boys began to cut and gather the cypress wood. This would be a long process to cut each board just the right size. They worked hard and seemed to enjoy the work more each day. After a few weeks, they began to see the shape of the boat taking place. It would be a magnificent structure when it was completed.

Meanwhile, across the great ocean lived Max and Millie Monkey. A pair of red-faced spider monkeys, the two had grown up together in the beautiful land they called home. Wherever you saw one, you saw the other.

As they grew older, they decided to become husband and wife, since they could not imagine life without each other.

"Millie, did you get the bananas we needed to make dinner with?" asked Max.

"Yes, dear. We have all the ingredients for banana casserole," answered Millie.

"You know it's my favorite. I could eat it every night," said Max.

"You do eat it every night, Max." Millie laughed.

Max and Millie always got out after dinner. They would swing from tree to tree, visiting with a few friends.

"It's such a beautiful place to live. Just look at all the flowers, Max," said Millie.

"Yes, it is. I never want to leave our beautiful home," answered Max.

"Hey, look, Millie. There's Eric and Alice Elephant. They're the nicest elephants in the jungle," said Max.

"Eric, my friend, how's it going? Were you able to go see the leopards and the lions race last week?" asked Max.

"Yes. It was the best race I've seen in a while," answered Eric. "They were neck and neck until the end, and the lion crossed the finish line by a nose. It was the upset of the year."

21

"Alice, you want to meet for lunch next week and go look at all the new flowers down by the water stream?" asked Millie.

"Girl, you know I do. I've been waiting for the big red and yellow flowers for weeks. I think they would look wonderful against my gray skin," answered Alice.

The two couples visited for a while and then went on their way. Max and Millie ran into their friends, Pat and Pete Panther, Bill and Cheryl Rabbit, and others while they were out.

"Well, dear, we should get back home before it gets dark," said Max.

Off the little monkeys went, swinging from tree to tree, until they reached home.

It was about noon the next day when Max and Millie heard a voice. It was a kind voice that asked them to listen carefully. "I am an angel sent by God to give you His message of the following instructions. In two days, you are to go to the waterfall in the jungle. There you will get the rest of the instructions God has for you," said the angel.

As fast as the angel appeared, he disappeared, leaving the little monkeys with many questions.

"Who is God? What is God?" asked Millie.

"I'm not sure, but do you remember when the humans came to the village north of the creek? I heard them talking about God. They said He created the world and everything in it in seven days. They said He was the creator of everything, including us. They said He was a good and loving God. I watched one of the humans talk to him on his knees. I had a feeling this was the real God, and I was glad I had learned about Him," Max told her, adding, "I don't think we should be afraid. I think we should be glad He came to us."

That afternoon, the Elephants, the Panthers, the Rabbits, and other couples from their area came to see Max and Millie. They had all received the same message from the angel. Max explained what he had heard from the humans and that there was nothing to fear.

According to their instructions, God had asked them all to meet at noon the following day by the waterfall in the jungle.

The time finally came for Max and Millie to go to the waterfall. They questioned what a God as great as this God could want with the animals. They would soon find out.

As they got closer to the falls, they saw all their friends coming. Eric and Alice came over to Max and Millie. "We're pretty nervous about this God thing," Eric told them. "We're not at all sure what's going on. It's a strange thing. God has only called male and female couples to come—and not all of them. It seems to be only one couple of each kind."

As the last couple came in by the falls, an angel appeared just in front of the waterfall. He was large and dressed in white clothes. His hair was gold, and his eyes sparkled like diamonds.

"I have been sent from God Most High. You have all been handpicked by God to go across the great ocean to the home of a man named Noah," said the angel.

24

"What are you talking about? How will we cross the great ocean? And why does God want us to do that?" shouted the animals.

"Please, calm down and listen. God has seen the earth He created and all the bad things in it. God has decided to clean the world with a flood. You will go to the man Noah in order to be safe. He and his sons have built a great ark for your safety from the flood. God will give Noah a sign when it is safe to come out of the ark. You leave the ark, and go back to your homes and multiply," instructed the angel.

Suddenly, the animals heard the voice of God. "Do not be afraid," He told them. "I will be with you and protect you. I am appointing Max and Millie as your leaders on this journey. I will give Max everything you need for this trip. He is a good monkey and will lead you well."

The angel told them to go home and be prepared to leave in three days. "You will meet on the banks of the large ocean and leave from there."

None of the animals understood what was happening, but all agreed that God did know, and they would obey Him.

The days passed quickly, and the animals met where the angel told them to be. They each carried a few personal things, and Alice and Millie made sure to bring lots of flowers in case they had to replant them. Alice vowed she had to have her red and yellow flowers that looked so amazing against her gray skin.

The angel was there as they gathered. "Let's go," said the angel.

"What do you mean, let's go?!" shouted Pat Panther.

"Yes, what do you mean? It's miles of deep water. How will we get across?" asked Larry Lion.

"You will have to trust that God will take care of you," replied the angel.

"Okay. I'll go first," said Max.

Max took Millie's hand and very cautiously took the first step onto the water. Immediately a long bridge began to form across the water. With each step, the

bridge extended until you could no longer see the
end. One after the other, each animal cautiously
stepped onto the wooden path across the great
ocean. It was the first steps of a long journey of faith
to a man named Noah.

Noah and his sons had been working on the ark for
many months. They had been laughed at, made fun
of, and called some very mean names. But they were
doing this for God, and none of that mattered.

They had finally reached the final steps of completing
the massive boat. The three decks were ready with
pins, stalls, and cages. All the food was kept near the
animals for easy feeding. Noah, Shem, Ham, Japheth,
and their wives each had their own room stocked
with things they would need.

"Well, Pop, it's almost finished, and I see the dark clouds the angel described that will bring the flood. What about the animals? There isn't enough time to go and herd them in. Pop, what about the dangerous animals? How will we ever get them into cages?" questioned Shem.

Just as they drove the last few nails, they heard a loud noise. Looking around, they saw all the animals coming toward them.

"Quick, Japheth, open the big door," said Noah.

Shem and Ham ran to help. They lowered the door, which also served as a ramp.

The animals calmly walked up the ramp. Each seemed to know exactly where to go. They went to their cages, pens, and stalls.

Of course, Noah and his sons did not see the band of angels leading them to their new homes.

Noah smiled as if he might have seen an angel. He knew that God keeps His promises, just as He was doing now.

As the rain began to fall, God told Noah and his family to enter the large boat, which was called an ark. Noah was six hundred years old when they entered the ark.

For forty days, the rain came down very hard, and the waters grew deeper. It rained until the big boat began to float.

One day, as Max and Millie were swinging across the rafters checking on all of their friends, the ark began to rock. "What's happening, Max?" cried Millie.

"I'm not sure, Millie. But I think God has sent a very strong wind," replied Max.

Shem, Ham, and Japheth grabbed on to the closest post and held on tightly. "What's going on? The wind is going to turn the boat over," shouted Japheth.

Noah walked from post to post, reassuring his sons and the animals that God would protect them and telling them to hold tight until it was over.

Not long after Noah spoke, the strong wind stopped. It was calm once again.

Max and Millie had been a great help to Noah, easily swinging across the ark in record time. They kept watch for any problems that might arise. They could go to the opening at the top of the boat to check for dry land.

Early one morning, just as the sun was coming up, Max checked the top windows.

"I see mountains," Max screamed.

After another forty days, Noah opened a window and released a raven. The bird flew back and forth until the waters began to dry up. Noah also released a dove. When it could not find a place to land, it came back. A few days later, he let the dove go out again. This time, it brought back a leaf.

They were very excited to see the leaf; it was almost time to open the doors and go home. You could hear cheers all across the boat.

Once again, the dove was released, and this time it never came back. After two more months, the grounds were finally dry.

God spoke to Noah. "Open the doors. Release the animals so they may go and multiply. And then you and your family may also leave the boat."

The big door slowly opened. You could hear the creaking in every part of the boat. The sun was blinding and beautiful. It was a glorious sight to see the earth again.

They all stopped and looked at the beautiful world God had created for them—grass greener than they had ever seen, trees with new leaves, flowers of every color. It was truly a glorious sight.

Alice screamed with excitement when she spotted her favorite flowers blooming—the ones that looked so amazing against her gray skin.

Max and Millie came to Noah with sad hearts. "We are going to miss you, Noah. It has been a real pleasure to be on this journey with you and your family," cried Max.

"I look forward to meeting again, my friends. May God bless you and all the little monkeys you are going to have," said Noah.

The animals begin the long journey back home. The bridge was there just as it had been before. Max and Millie led the way home.

Noah and his family built an altar to God before they did anything else. There they worshiped the Lord with a burnt offering of their best animals and birds.

Once again, God spoke to Noah. "Noah, I am pleased with your altar and sacrifice. I will never again flood the whole world. As long as the earth remains, there will be planting and harvesting. There will be cold, heat, summer, winter, day, and night." God blessed Noah and his family. "This is my promise to you and all who come after you," he said. "I am giving you a sign that will always remind you of my promise."

"Papa, Papa, look in the sky!" shouted Shem.

There in the sky, from one end of the earth to the other, was a large rainbow, with bright colors—red, orange, yellow, green, blue, indigo, and purple in a perfect half-moon shape.

Max, Millie and the other animals saw the beautiful rainbow. They knew it must be from the God who loved them and had kept them safe just as He had promised.

Max looked at Millie with his warm smile. "God always keeps His promise, Millie, and I'm glad we had the chance to be a part of His plan."

They watched the beautiful rainbow until it disappeared and then continued their journey back home.

Gus and the Lion's Den

Gus was a young lion who lived with his parents, Sadie and Bo. Their family lived in the Palace of King Darius. Gus was the oldest of three. He had a younger sister, Katie, and a little brother, Nate (short for Nathan). They were a happy family with all the luxuries of life.

King Darius made sure they were well cared for by some of his top soldiers. There was John, a big soldier who showed little affection for the family. He brought their food and water and always seemed annoyed. Then there was Peter, a thin tall soldier who sang and whistled all the time. But Gus's favorite was a small soldier named Rodney. Rodney came most days because he truly loved their lion family. He talked to the lions as if they were his best friends.

Rodney and Gus formed a bond so strong that Gus would eat treats from his hand.

Rodney had to keep his friendship a secret from the other soldiers. King Darius had made it clear that the lions had one purpose, and it was not to be friends with any humans.

Gus didn't know what their purpose was, and he really didn't care. He just enjoyed playing with his little brother, Nate, and watching the soldiers march.

Gus's den was by the grounds where the soldiers lived. He would often lie quietly and listen to their conversations. He heard them often speak of a man named Daniel.

"Daniel is always in the right, according to the king," said Peter, adding, "I'm getting tired of the king giving him the best jobs that should be ours."

"I agree," said John. "He's not even one of us. He's a captive from Judah."

Gus listened closely, hoping to learn why they all hated Daniel so much. They never revealed any bad qualities about Daniel, he was a hard worker, smart, and always obedient to the king. Daniel, from all accounts, did his best at everything he was asked to do.

Gus loved to hear the stories of Daniel and his ability to understand dreams. This fascinated Gus, and he became very fond of Daniel, even though he had never met him.

He learned from the soldiers' stories that Daniel was responsible for their menu being changed from meat, bread, pastries, and wine to healthier foods, such as fruits, vegetables, and water. This did not sit well with most of the soldiers. And all, except for Rodney, wanted to see Daniel dead. Rodney knew that Daniel's God was the one true God. Rodney saw that the soldiers became stronger, faster, and even smarter from eating Daniel's diet. Rodney had also asked Daniel's God to be his God. He understood Daniel's love and obedience to their God.

Gus waited every day to hear the soldier's stories of complaints about Daniel and his friends. The soldiers, as well as others under King Darius, were so jealous that they became obsessed with trying to get rid of them.

Gus's favorite story was the story of Daniel's friends Shadrach, Meshach, and Abednego. It was said that every day the boys prayed and worshiped only to their God in heaven. This was during the time of King Nebuchadnezzar, long before Gus was born.

The king had a ninety-foot gold statue of himself placed in the province of Babylon. He sent a message—at the sound of the musical instruments, all the people were to bow before the statue of King Nebuchadnezzar and worship it. Anyone who did not worship the statue would be thrown into the fiery furnace.

The high officials thought they had the perfect plan to get rid of Daniel's friends Shadrach, Meshach, and Abednego forever. "They will not bow down to that statue," said one of the officials. "And the king will have no choice but to put them to death."

Gus waited to hear the best part of the story. He loved the part where Shadrach, Meshach, and Abednego did refuse to bow down to another god, as they told the king that their God would always take care of them.

Wow, thought Gus. *I sure wish I could meet their God.*

Come on. Finish the story, he thought.

Finally, the soldiers picked up the story again and told how the king had to become so angry with the three boys that he'd heated the furnace seven times hotter than usual.

"Throw them in!" shouted the king.

The three friends were cast into the burning furnace as ordered.

"Soldier, you did put only three men in the furnace?" the king asked.

"Yes, Great King. Only three men were thrown into the fire," answered the soldier.

"But I see four," said the king. "Who is the fourth man?"

"Shadrach, Meshach, and Abednego, come out!" ordered the king.

They came from the fiery furnace without even having their clothes singed.

"Yahoo!" roared Gus. "I love that part."

"Gus, come on in. I see Rodney coming with dinner," shouted Mom.

Gus thought of Daniel and his friends often. He knew that they were special, and he knew it was because of their love and devotion to their God.

One day, as Gus was strolling around his large pen, a man came up and spoke to him gently. "Hello, boy. What's your name?" asked the nice man. "I watch you every day from my window. You seem to enjoy the stories of the soldiers. I can see you are a smart and sensitive lion. You are a beautiful creation of the Lord.

"Oh, my name is Daniel," the man added. "Who might I have the privilege of speaking to?"

Gus growled softly.

And Daniel smiled as if he understood. "I'll call you Gus the Listener."

Gus could hardly believe his eyes. It was really Daniel. He didn't look at all mean or dangerous as the guards had described him. It was just the opposite. He was gentle and kind and had something special about him that Gus couldn't describe. *I think he has peace,* thought Gus. No one other than Rodney seemed to possess this quality.

That night, Gus was sure that Rodney and Daniel had a special love and peace because of the God they worshiped. He wondered if their God could also become his God as well.

Several years passed, and Gus still was not sure of his purpose to the king.

The officials continued trying to get rid of Daniel, and as always, Daniel's God protected him. Gus would smile as he grew more in love with Daniel's Great God.

It was a warm day as Gus lay listening to the soldiers when he heard his family's name mentioned. Gus moved closer to the gate, hoping to hear more.

He overheard another plot to have Daniel put to death, and this time it would involve him.

"No, I can't do what they're expecting of me. I can't kill Daniel," cried Gus. "I don't care how hungry I am or even if the king puts me to death. I will not kill Daniel."

The plot was a simple one and was sure to end Daniel's life.

This was the plan. The high officials would go to King Darius and tell him that all the country should worship only him, for he was the only great king. The high officials would tell him that, for the next thirty days, any person who prayed to anyone or anything except him would be thrown into the lion's den.

After they had visited the king with this suggestion, the governors, high officials, and administrators bowed and said, "Long live King Darius."

King Darius puffed up with pride and gladly signed the decree.

Many days passed, and over this time, Gus and his family were not fed.

"Dad, we are so hungry, why aren't they feeding us?" asked Gus.

Gus's dad began to tell him what their real purpose was to the king.

"No. I don't think I can do such a thing, "cried Gus.

"You have to, son. It is our way. We are wild animals, and the king is in control. If you do not obey, the king will have us all killed," said his dad.

Gus went to his little straw bed in the corner. He no longer felt hungry. *I know,* thought Gus. *I'll pray to Daniel's God. If this is the true God, He will hear me. I know He will.*

A peace came over Gus after he talked to Daniel's God, and he felt as though He might be his God, too.

The sunlight of a new day warmed Gus's back as he woke, only to remember today was the day he was to kill Daniel.

Gus gathered his family around. "I have to tell you about Daniel and his God." Gus shared his reasons for not wanting to kill Daniel. He told them that he thought that Daniel's God was the only real God.

"I'm not so sure about all this, Gus. But we will see what happens," said Dad.

Bo was a good Dad and wanted the best for his family. He knew they had to obey the king, or it was sure death for all of them.

"Okay, here's the plan. They will lower the man, Daniel, down to our den. We will all begin to smell the aroma of this human. Don't attack at first. Just walk slowly around him enjoying the delicious smell of dinner. Then I will attack first, followed by Gus and Nate. After he is dead, we will all enjoy a feast, and the king will reward us with great meals forever," explained Gus's dad.

Gus asked once again for Daniel's God to come and save them all.

The rope that tightly held Daniel began slowly lowering him closer and closer to the ground. Bo clawed at the ground preparing to attack. Nate was so hungry he started toward Daniel with his teeth and claws, ready to destroy.

That's when it happened! An angel sent from Daniel's God appeared. "Lions, move back and sit quietly," said the angel. "The True God, the God of Daniel and Creator of all things, has sent me to protect him and you."

The lions were terrified and quickly obeyed the angel.

"God Most High has ordered that your mouths be shut."

At that moment, neither Gus nor any of his family could open their mouths—well, except that Gus somehow managed a smile as he looked at Daniel.

Gus got down on his two front paws and bowed before God. He thanked Him for protecting Daniel and his family. He asked if He would be his God also.

The angel came over to Gus, rubbed his head, and told him God had heard his prayer, and He was Lord to everyone who asked Him.

King Darius rushed out the next morning, hoping Daniel's God had protected him. "Daniel, has your God saved you?" asked King Darius.

Daniel answered, "Long live the king. My God sent an angel and shut the mouths of the lions, for I am innocent in His sight. I have not harmed you, Your Majesty."

King Darius was overjoyed as he saw that Daniel was unharmed.

He knew Daniel's God was the true God and ordered all the kingdom to worship only Daniel's God.

Daniel prospered during the reign of King Darius, and so did Gus and his family.

Delmer and the Good Shepherd

Delmer was a small lamb in a flock of about a hundred other sheep. Many of the sheep were his relatives. There was Mama, Papa, Uncle Joe, Aunt Sarah, Grandpa, Grandma, and many cousins. The sheep led a quiet, peaceful life. They were also resourceful and never forgot a face, especially if it belonged to a goat.

On the other side of the great forest lived a herd of goats. You might not think much of that—unless you were a sheep. You see, sheep and goats had never gotten along.

"Those blasted goats are nothing but trouble," Papa would always say. As long as Delmer could remember, he had been told to stay away from them.

Delmer, like all the lambs, attended class at Little Lamb Elementary. Mr. Roberts, the teacher, was a large older ram. He was graying on his forehead and quite large in size. He was soft-spoken and very wise. Mr. Roberts always preached how a sheep's only protection was staying together! He told stories about sheep that had strayed away from their herd. He told the lambs that the enemy was always around waiting. "Oh, the enemy is patient and sometimes may even look like another sheep," he would say.

The lambs would swallow hard with fear as Mr. Roberts continued the stories.

"Another group you should be aware of are those wild, out-of-control, pesky goats! Just the thought of them makes my wool itch. They have no boundaries and always seem to cause trouble. I guess they're not really our enemy, but they're just not like us. So stay away from them, or they'll take you down the wrong path for sure," said Mr. Roberts.

"What's the wrong path, Mr. Roberts?" Bobby asked.

"Glad you asked. Let's back up a little," said Mr. Roberts. "You, young friends, have a Good Shepherd. He is the one who watches over us at all times, day and night. He protects us from our enemies. He

50

also leads us to the green, yummy grass. The Good Shepherd knows each one of you by name. He even knows the sound of your voice. You will learn the sound of His voice the more you get to know Him. He is the one who leads us to the great pen at night and guards the gate with his life. He is the one who makes sure we have what we need.

"He also gives us rules to obey. The main rule is to learn the sound of His voice. The next rule is to obey what He tells us to do. You see, little lambs, He sees the dangers we face, and He knows what is best for us. No one will ever care for you like the Good Shepherd does. One day he will take us to a home where there will be no more enemies and where the grass and water will never run out—a place you can roam without fear."

"Oh boy, Mr. Roberts, when can we go? I'm ready," said Bobby.

"No one knows when He will take us," said Mr. Roberts. "I do know there is only one path to get there, and the Good Shepherd is the only one who can take you there. It is a place for any animal who chooses to follow the Good Shepherd."

Delmer had lots of friends, but his two best friends were Abby and Bobby. They looked forward to running and playing every day.

"Bobby, do you think the goats are as bad as everyone says?" Delmer asked.

"I don't know and don't really care," said Bobby.

"Well, they say they've never even heard about the Good Shepherd. I've also heard they will eat and drink anything that doesn't move," said Abby.

"Oh, come on, Abby. How is that even possible," said Bobby.

"Oh, it's possible! Trust me. Sadie told me she heard from Jasper that one night they got into old Farmer Amos's yard and ate every one of the sheets hanging on the clothesline," said Abby.

"Abby, what did you mean they've never heard of the Good Shepherd?" asked Delmer. "Everyone has heard of the Good Shepherd!"

"Not the goats. They want nothing to do with Him."

"Billy's friend Jim told him that, once, another man said he was the Good Shepherd and told them things that were not true, and the goats believed him. I've heard they've been crazy ever since," replied Abby.

Delmer thought about the goats that night. He wondered why no one had ever told them the truth about the Good Shepherd. He thought of the glorious home that the Good Shepherd had prepared for them. He also remembered what Mr. Roberts had said about how any animal could go if he or she choses to obey and follow the Good Shepherd. It broke Delmer's heart that others had told lies about his Good Shepherd.

I have to go tell the goats about the truth, thought Delmer.

Delmer snuggled down between Mama and Papa that night. He felt warm and safe knowing the Good Shepherd was watching over them. He couldn't help but feel sad that the goats would never know this safe feeling unless someone told them the good news of the Good Shepherd.

Delmer knew what he had to do. He lay awake most of the night planning his getaway. The goats deserved to know the truth, and Delmer had every intention of telling them.

The next morning, Delmer, Bobby, and Abby headed to school. "I have to tell you all something," said Delmer.

"What are you planning now?" Bobby asked.

"I'm going to go tell the goats about the Good Shepherd," said Delmer.

"What! You can't be serious! You know you can't leave the herd. It's much too dangerous," cried Abby.

Bobby joined in, telling Delmer it was a crazy idea and that he could get hurt, or worse, killed.

"I know it will be dangerous, but I have given it a lot of thought and I think it's what I'm supposed to do." replied Delmer.

Both friends gave in and agreed that even though it was dangerous, the goats deserved to know the truth.

Delmer's plan was set, and with Bobby and Abby's help, he would leave the next morning before the others woke up.

He stayed awake most of the night, afraid of the enemy and a little afraid of the goats.

Delmer woke early and gently eased himself from his warm bed, careful not to wake Mama and Papa.

He quietly walked in the direction of the great forest. He was all alone now, and the sounds of his teacher's voice rang in his ears. *Never go off alone.* Delmer looked around for signs of the enemy, but it was quiet, and he moved on.

Suddenly, he heard a noise in the brush up ahead of him. He stopped, and when he no longer heard it, he moved on. As he came up on a thorn bush along the path, a small creature jumped out in front of him. Delmer screamed and looked for a place to hide, his mind racing with fear that the enemy had found him, only to realize it was just an old badger.

"What you are doing in these here woods all alone, boy?" the old badger asked. "Is you crazy or something? Don't you know that ole enemy is a waiting fer a little sheep such as yourself?"

"Yes, sir, I do know. But I'm on a mission, and it was a chance I had to take," said Delmer.

"Well, I reckon you is crazy as them there goats in the next field." With that last comment, the badger scampered off into the forest.

It took Delmer a few minutes to get his courage back, but soon after he was off again.

He began to hear the goats as he made his way through the forest. *Am I doing the right thing?* He began to question his decision. It was too late now. He had come too far to go back.

As he entered the place where the goats lived, he realized that, in a lot of ways, they were like the sheep. They had families and friends. They needed food and water just like the sheep did. They also needed the Good Shepherd.

Their life fascinated Delmer. He had never been outside of his herd. The goats were scattered all over the fields, and their behavior was very different from that of the sheep. They were loud and rowdy and didn't seem to have any rules.

"Okay," said Delmer, "here I go." Although he was nervous and had no plan, he did have a message, and it was his duty to share it.

Some of the goats stared at him, wondering why he was there. His first encounter was with two older goats. "What you are doing here, boy?" the goats asked.

Delmer, stuttering a little, answered, "I-I came to tell you about the Good Shepherd."

"Why did you do that?" the goats answered.

"Well, because the Good Shepherd is loving and kind, and He is the only one who can lead you to the glorious home He has prepared for any animal who chooses to follow Him. I wanted you to know the truth," stuttered Delmer.

"Well, we don't want to follow you or your shepherd! You sheep have made it clear that if we don't become just like you, we are not welcome in your herd or in that shepherd's herd either. Now you get out of here, and take your message with you! We are happy with our lives, and that's all that matters! We like things just the way they are," shouted the goats.

"You don't understand," cried Delmer. "Without the Good Shepherd's truth, you're going to end up in the home of the enemy forever. You will be away from His love and His protective hand. What could be worse than being separated from the Shepherd?"

The goats laughed at Delmer and made fun of his message.

Delmer slowly walked away, feeling like he had failed the Good Shepherd and that he had also failed the goats. *I thought everyone would want to follow the Good Shepherd if they knew the truth.* This would be a lesson that Delmer would never forget.

He had begun to make his way back to the safety of his little herd, when he heard a voice behind him. "Wait. Stop. I want to talk to you."

Delmer looked back and saw a young goat running toward him. "I heard you talking to those other goats back in the meadow. Is it true what you said? Oh, sorry. My name is Gary."

Delmer looked at Gary and wondered if he really wanted to know the truth or if he was just trying to make him feel like a failure. "I need to get going. I have a long way to go," said Delmer.

"Okay, I guess it's not important, or you would tell me," said Gary.

Delmer stopped, looked back, and answered, "It's true! The Good Shepherd is the only one who knows the right path to His home."

"Do you think I could meet Him? The Good Shepherd I mean," asked Gary.

"Sure. He would love to meet you," said Delmer.

So off they went, each from different lifestyles and different teaching, yet both would have to make the same choice in life.

Delmer was nervous about what the other sheep would say. Some of the sheep felt the goats had to change first, or they would not fit in the herd. Delmer thought they should be loved first, or they would never understand who the Good Shepherd was.

Delmer had his work cut out for him. The Good Shepherd had a message for the sheep, as well as the goats.

Gary and Delmer were almost back home when they heard the sound of a mountain lion. "We'll never make it back to my herd. What should we do? He's getting closer," cried Delmer.

"Let's hide. Maybe he won't see us," said Gary. They found a big rock and ducked down!

Delmer wished the Good Shepherd knew where he was. He closed his eyes and prayed. "Please come save us, Good Shepherd."

If only I had told you where I was going, thought Delmer.

Gary watched Delmer carefully, wondering if his shepherd was real. Gary remembered others who had said they were shepherds, only to lead some of the goats to dark places that separated them from their families.

The mountain lion was getting closer!

"He can smell us. He's going to find us," whispered Gary.

They got close together and closed their eyes. They could hear the lion's growl getting closer and closer!

Just then, Gary jumped out to confront the lion. "Run, Delmer. Go back to your herd. I'll fight him long enough for you to get home safe," shouted Gary.

"No, Gary. We'll fight him together," said Delmer.

Both little animals stood their ground. The mountain lion roared loudly and charged! Delmer was ready for a fight he knew he would lose.

Suddenly, as the lion leaped toward them, he fell to the ground.

"What happened? Do you think we scared him to death?" asked Gary.

"I don't think so," said Delmer.

"Look. He was hit in the head with this rock," said Gary.

The two little animals stood there, afraid to move. And then they felt the gentle touch of a hand. It was the Good Shepard.

"You came for me!" said Delmer. "How did you know where I was?"

"Oh, little one. I always know where you are. I knew the morning you left with my message for the goats. Thank you for telling them that I love them," said the Good Shepherd.

Gary knew Delmer had told him the truth, and he wondered if the Good Shepherd could love him. Gary lowered his head, with tears running down his face. He bowed down before the Good Shepherd and asked if he could follow Him. "I want to obey your rules because now I know you are truth. I see now that you know what's best for me. You give me a happiness that's different from any I've ever felt. I don't want to lose that! But I'm not a very good little goat, I've done a lot of things that were wrong," said Gary.

The Good Shepherd smiled and pulled Gary close. "Your wrong choices have already been paid for, little one. Gary, I have always known you, just as I have always known Delmer. You just didn't know that. I have always loved you, and I've hoped that, one day, you would want to follow me. You see, Gary. I had to let you choose to come to me. I was always there.

"Your choice to follow me makes you part of my flock—and Delmer's new brother."

Gary loved being part of this new family.

He would teach the sheep about his lifestyle as a goat and why the goats didn't want to be part of their herd.

Gary, Delmer, Bobby, and Abby became the best of friends. They loved going to school and learning all about the Good Shepherd's love for them.

One day while walking home from school, Gary told his friends he was going back to his meadow to the goats he loved.

"No. You can't go back there. You're not like them anymore, and they might be mean to you," cried Abby.

Delmer and Bobby agreed.

"Please don't go. We'll miss you too much!" said Bobby.

Gary stopped them and told them he had been having long conversations with the Good Shepherd. "He told me it was time for me to go back and tell them the truth," explained Gary, adding, "I love them, and I want them to know what I know!"

Bobby, Abby, and Delmer knew it was the right thing, even though they wanted Gary to stay.

Gary said goodbye the next morning and headed home. Abby cried. Delmer wanted to cry but fought not to. Bobby felt sad for the first time in his life.

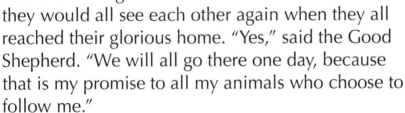

Later that day, the Good Shepherd comforted them. He told them that Gary would be all right and they would all see each other again when they all reached their glorious home. "Yes," said the Good Shepherd. "We will all go there one day, because that is my promise to all my animals who choose to follow me."

That night, as Delmer lay down between his parents, he felt happy that he had gotten to know Gary and looked forward to seeing his friend again.

He thanked the Good Shepherd for His promise and for loving him.

He closed his eyes and went to sleep, wondering if the Good Shepherd would send him on another mission. If so, he was ready. And maybe this time, Abby and Bobby would come along.

Part Two

I love those who love me, and those who seek me diligently find me.

—*Proverbs 8:17 (ESV)*

Jedediah's Lunch

"Jedediah," called his mom, "time for dinner."

Jedediah and Abel stopped their game of hide-and-seek and headed toward home.

"See you tomorrow, Jedediah," shouted Abel.

Jedediah ran in the house, starving as usual.

Jedediah was eleven years old and growing like a weed, as his mother always said. All he knew was he stayed hungry, and there never seemed to be enough food to fill him up.

Jedediah had two older brothers, Jesse and Jude. He also had a little sister, Sarah. Sarah loved Jedediah and always wanted him to play with her. She was annoying at times. But overall, she was a good little sister.

His father, Micah, was a fisherman by trade. Magda, his mother, stayed home to care for the family and work their small garden. They also had a few goats and chickens.

Jedediah knew what it was to be hungry. He had experienced it several times before.

When Micah had successful fishing trips, they ate well. And Magda always dried and cured some of the fish for the hard times. The old goat gave them milk when she was fed regularly. Magda always fed the children first, and she and Micah ate last.

Jedediah loved to go into Bethsaida with his dad while he looked for boats that were hiring. His dad was well known as a smart and hardworking fisherman. He was first hired if there were jobs.

On this particular day Jedediah was ambling around town waiting for his dad. He heard people talking excitedly about a great prophet who was traveling around preaching and healing the sick.

Jedediah became intrigued with this prophet, Jesus. *Who was he?*

Abel's cousin Andrew had given up everything to follow him. He had told them that Jesus was God's Son and that he had come to offer lasting life with God for all who accept Him.

70

Jedediah listened closely to stories about people being healed and great miracles being performed, *could he be the one who Isaiah told about in the Bible Scroll?*

Jedediah's dad often read the Bible scroll at night, and he remembered him reading about a Messiah who would come.

Jedediah really just liked the stories about David and Goliath; Daniel and the lion's den; and, his favorite, the talking donkey.

Jedediah found his dad, and off they went for home.

"Did you find a job, Dad?" asked Jedediah. "I sure hope so. Food is getting low at home, and Mother's garden hasn't done well without rain."

"I know, son. But no job today. Maybe tomorrow," said his father.

Jedediah saw the sadness and fear on his dad's face, and it scared him a little.

The next day, Jedediah and Abel met as usual. They played a few games and soon became bored. "I know," said Abel. "Let's make slingshots. We could use them to hunt with. Let's go look for the right tree to get some bark for our slings.

We won't need much, and we can always find scraps of leather lying around."

"Wow, that sounds great. I can be David, and that big old tree can be Goliath. I'll show him who's boss." Jedediah laughed.

The boys eagerly started their quest to make the perfect sling.

"Let's go down toward the river where all those big trees are," suggested Jedediah. "We'll be able to get all the bark we need."

The boys found the perfect tree and began stripping the bark. They soon had enough for two slings. Once they found a comfortable place to sit and work, they began the process of weaving the stripped bark. It would take a while to weave the thin strips tight enough to be strong. They didn't mind. It was a good time to laugh and talk. The boys talked about a lot of things. They always did. That's what made their friendship so special. They could tell each other just about anything.

"Abel, do you believe the things that your cousin Andrew said about Jesus?" asked Jedediah.

"I sure do. I saw him become a changed man. He walked away from his old life to follow Jesus," said Abel.

"I don't get it. I believe in God. Is there more to it than that?" asked Jedediah.

"Andrew says that we can't get to God unless we believe Jesus really is God's Son—something about faith. I don't know everything, Jedediah. I heard Jesus is near us in other towns preaching, and He may even come here," said Abel.

"Oh, I hope so. I would very much like to meet Him and find that hope everyone's talking about," said Jedediah.

"I think my bark is ready. Let's go find some leather for the pocket and smooth sling rocks," said Abel.

The boys worked the rest of the day on their slingshots. It was getting dark and they decided to finish them the next day.

Jedediah made it home just in time for dinner.

"Oh no, not potatoes and water again, Mother," cried Jedediah.

"Jedediah, you stop that," his mother scolded. "We are fortunate to have this. There are people without any food at all tonight."

"I'm sorry, Mother. You're right," said Jedediah.

"Let's give God thanks for providing us with food tonight," said his dad.

Micah and Magda always gave thanks for what they had.

Somehow, those old potatoes tasted pretty good, and Jedediah felt full and happy.

Jedediah and his brothers played, while Mother combed and braided little Sarah's hair.

"Time for bible reading. Come, children. Sit on the floor while I read," said his dad.

He read from Psalm 147:11. "The Lord delights in those who fear him, who put their hope in his unfailing love."

"Dad, do you know of the man, Jesus?" asked Jedediah.

"Yes, I do. And I hear he is coming close to Bethsaida to preach tomorrow. I think it would be nice if we went to listen to what he has to say," answered his dad.

"Is he the Messiah, Dad?" asked Jedediah.

"Yes, I believe he is," answered his dad.

"What does that mean?" asked Jedediah. "I don't really understand."

"Well, do you remember in the Bible scroll where Isaiah tells us a child will be born and they will call His name Immanuel? He tells us again in another passage that he will be called Wonder, Counselor, Mighty God, Everlasting Father, and Prince of Peace. He will bear the sins of all and bring a new covenant. He will be the door to God the Father and the only way to get to Him," said his dad, adding, "God sent his Son to us. I'm not sure how He will bear our sins. But I'm afraid He will have to suffer and die in our place. "Jedediah, I do believe Jesus is God's Son." answered his dad.

"Jedediah, just as Andrew gave it all to follow Him, that is what He wants from all of us," continued his dad.

"Oh, Father, I hope I see Jesus tomorrow."

"I hope so too, son," answered his dad.

Jedediah had a hard time going to sleep. All he could think of was that Jesus the Messiah, God's own Son, would be near them.

Jedediah hit the floor before daylight the next morning, asking if he could go early and get a good place. "I don't want breakfast. I'm too excited to eat," he said.

"Wait, Jedediah. I will fix you a basket to take. I have fresh barley bread and cured fish," said his mother.

"Oh, hurry, Mother. I'm going to be late and miss Jesus," cried Jedediah.

"Here are five loaves of bread and two fish so you won't get hungry. There's enough to share with friends," said his mother.

Jedediah took off as crowds were already gathering. Jedediah saw Andrew, Abel's cousin. "Andrew, may I come stay with you until my family gets here?" asked Jedediah.

"Sure. Come on. We have a lot to do, and I could use the help," said Andrew.

Jedediah and Andrew walked around helping the people to find places to sit. The disciples were kind as they welcomed everyone to hear Jesus.

Suddenly, Philip and John came running over to Andrew. They seemed very worried. They began to explain that the people had been following Jesus for a long time. When Jesus looked out at them, he felt compassion because they had not eaten in a while. He asked us to feed them.

"What shall we do? We don't have enough food or money to feed this many people. There has to be at least five thousand men and their families here," said Philip.

"You can have my lunch. There are five loaves of fresh barley bread and two cured fish," boasted Jedediah.

Philip laughed, and John smiled. But Andrew said that Jedediah had great faith and kindness.

"Come with me Jedediah," said Andrew.

Up the hill they walked. When they reached the top, Jedediah saw a man praying. He had a kindness Jedediah could feel even before He looked at him.

"Is that Jesus?" asked Jedediah.

"Yes, it is," answered Andrew.

Jedediah found himself kneeling down in front of Him.

"Jedediah, I am so happy you came to see me," said Jesus.

"You know my name?" asked Jedediah.

"I do. I knew you before your mother did. I also know your heart, and it is pleasing to me." Jesus smiled.

"Philip and John said you were worried that all the people would get hungry. I brought you my lunch to share with them. It's not much, but I want to give it all to you, Jesus. I do believe you are God's Son, and I want to follow you just like Andrew," said Jedediah.

"Jedediah, when you give your all to me, you become a part of my family. Welcome. I will never leave you," said Jesus.

"Oh, wow, Jedediah. You are now my little brother in Christ," said Andrew

"I think I would like to be baptized, Andrew. Would you baptize me?" asked Jedediah.

"I would be honored to, little brother," replied Andrew.

Jedediah had a warm, safe feeling of peace he had never experienced before. He now understood— giving Christ his all and seeing Jesus as God's Son was what salvation meant.

As Jesus stood to speak, a silence fell over the people.

"I want to feed your bodies and your soul today. Please enjoy the food shared by my friend and brother, Jedediah," said Jesus.

Jesus raised the little basket of food toward the heavens and gave God the praise and thanks for it.

The disciples began passing out the food, which never ran out. Everyone ate until they were satisfied. There were even twelve baskets of leftovers.

Then Jesus replied, "I am the bread of life. Whoever comes to me will never be hungry again." (John 6:35). "I tell you the truth, anyone who believes has eternal life." (John 6:47).

It was a day Jedediah would never forget. He became a part of the family of Christ. He had changed that day.

But after all, that's what happens when we meet Jesus.

Thaddeus the Israelite

"Thaddeus, Thaddeus, come on. Let's go for a swim," yelled Seth. Seth knew his best friend was probably hidden somewhere up on the hills playing his horn trumpet.

Thaddeus had been spending a lot of time playing his new trumpet.

When he was born, his father had taken the horn from of a ram and had begun the long process of making a trumpet for his son. It was a magnificent instrument, one of a kind. He had carved much of the journey of their people, along with some of their tribal history.

When Thaddeus turned twelve, his dad gave the beautiful horn trumpet to him. It was the beginning of a whole new love for him.

Even though the two boys were growing up, they still enjoyed laughing and playing games. Sometimes they would sneak down by the riverbanks of the Jordan and cut vines for the raft they were working on. They had great plans to sail down the river and see all the places they had heard about.

Thaddeus and Seth were great friends and had been as long as they could remember.

Thaddeus's dad was Andrew, son of Ezra. He was a high official in their tribe. There were twelve different tribes. Each had its own leader, but the tribes were all under the direction of Moses.

Thaddeus often stayed awake at night to listen to his mom and dad's conversations. There were a lot of people who had lost faith that they would ever see the Promised Land. They began to worship other gods and participate in sinful acts that broke God's heart. Thaddeus's parents were very concerned for their people.

It was a beautiful afternoon, with a cool crisp breeze as the sun was going down. Seth and Thaddeus had worked most of the day on their raft. They had just started covering it when they heard the trumpet call for all the tribes to come together at the high rock.

The boys quickly headed home to join their families. When all the tribes were called together, it usually meant that Moses was going to speak.

"What do you think is going on, Seth?" asked Thaddeus.

"I don't know, but it must be important. Maybe we are fixing to enter the Promise Land," said Thaddeus.

The boys found their families and gathered with the others to hear their great leader, Moses.

Joshua came to the high rock where Moses always spoke and addressed the people. "It is with great sadness that I tell you God has called Moses home. God has spoken to me. I will now lead you to the land that He has promised us. We are all hurt and, I'm sure, afraid. Please remember, Moses knew this was the way it would be. He knew he would never enter the Promised Land. I want to reassure you that the same great God who led Moses is also leading me," Joshua told them.

The people began to cry at the loss of their great leader, Moses. It was a dark day for the Israelites.

Thaddeus and his parents returned home that afternoon without much conversation. He could see his parents had great concerns, as well as being sad.

Thaddeus's mother, Hannah, was the daughter of Abel, a well-known prophet among their tribe. She was kind and gentle. Hannah was the one called when tragedy happened.

Thaddeus felt a lump rise in his throat and a feeling of fear.

His mom comforted him and reassured him that all this was part of God's great plan. "This is when you learn to trust God, Thaddeus," said his mom.

It would be up to Thaddeus's father to speak to the people of their tribe and calm their fears.

Thaddeus had never seen his father cry, but today, he shed many tears for his leader, friend, and mentor.

It would be a long night as Andrew met with other tribal leaders. Together they would prepare their speeches.

At sunrise, Thaddeus's tribe gathered on the bank of the Jordan River.

The water was so peaceful that morning that Thaddeus could see his full reflection.

What could his dad possibly say that would comfort their people? Thaddeus could see his dad's fear. He closed his eyes and prayed. *Please, God, give my dad the right words to say.*

Andrew started his speech quoting the Bible scroll. "The Lord himself goes before you and will be with you; He will never leave you nor forsake you. Do not be afraid; do not be discouraged."

"This is the word of the Lord. Joshua, son of Nun of the tribe Ephraim, was loved by Moses, served under him, and was chosen by God. He is obedient and does only as God instructs him. You have no reason to fear this change. We will see great and wonderful things through Joshua's leadership, for he is great in the eyes of our Lord."

A calmness fell over the people. They trusted Andrew and respected his judgement. If Andrew loved Joshua, so would they.

As time passed, the people became accustomed to Joshua and began to trust him.

Thaddeus and Seth continued to work on their raft while making great plans for their journey.

Thaddeus still used most of his free time to practice his trumpet, which he had gotten quite good at.

One day as he was playing, Joshua heard him.

"That's very good, young man. What's your name?" asked Joshua.

"I'm Thaddeus, son of Andrew," boasted Thaddeus.

"Well, that is some very fine music you're playing—every bit as good as the priests who play the horn trumpets," said Joshua.

Thaddeus beamed with excitement to have such a compliment given him by their leader, Joshua.

As Thaddeus headed home that day, he began to think of his future. Everyone including his parents felt he would follow in his father's footsteps and become a soldier. His heart, however, was filled with music and words of poetry. He would have to keep these feelings tucked away. *When you are the son of a warrior, you are also expected to become one,* thought Thaddeus.

Thaddeus and Seth met early the next morning to continue working on their raft. They played more than they worked, but that's what made getting together so much fun.

They were just getting ready to jump into the river for a swim when, once again, they heard the loud sound of the trumpet summoning everyone back to the great rock.

Joshua carefully took his place at the top to speak. "As you all know, we have been waiting to cross the river. God has given me a message," he announced. "Please listen to these words, for this is the Word of the Lord.

"The time has come to take the people across the Jordan River. Your tribe leaders are to gather their people. They will have three days to pack their belongings for the journey."

There was a great cheer among the people as they hurried to get ready to make the long-awaited trip.

Thaddeus and Seth sat down and smiled, as they remembered what their parents had taught them. "Have faith in the promise of our Great God. He always fulfills His promises."

Something changed in Thaddeus that day. He began to see God in a different way. He realized how much God loved them and that His plan and timing were perfect. Thaddeus was growing up.

From that day on he not only took his trumpet, but also his Bible scroll to his private place. There he would play his music to honor God, who had blessed him with this talent. He could hardly wait each day for his special time with God.

It was beginning to get dark as Thaddeus and his dad arrived home. "Hi, Dad, bet I can beat you to the front door," Thaddeus laughed.

"Not today, son," said Andrew.

Thaddeus could tell his dad looked troubled as he asked the family to sit and listen to what he had to say. "Joshua has asked me to take on a very important job. I can't tell you all the details, except it will be dangerous, and my life could be in danger. Thaddeus, I want you to take care of your mother while I'm away. Get the firewood and water. Make sure you keep my bow and arrows by the door. There's an old wolf that's been sniffing around, and I don't want him going after the livestock," said Andrew.

Thaddeus and his mother sat quietly without asking too many questions. They both knew that Andrew was the top warrior of all tribes, and it was his job and duty to obey Joshua.

The next night, Andrew was to meet in Joshua's tent with the others involved in the mission. Thaddeus couldn't stand it and followed his father. He just had to know what his father would be facing.

He eased around to the back of the tent, crawling slowly until he found a small opening he could see through. There he saw Joshua, an army general, his dad, and two other men who Thaddeus didn't know.

Joshua was praying over his dad and the other men. It felt like a sacred moment, and Thaddeus felt guilty intruding on it.

Joshua then turned the conversation over to the general, who would give his dad his instructions.

He held his breath, afraid of being caught and also afraid of what he would hear.

The two men from Shittim were to go as spies and look over the land and city of Jericho. They were to go to the home of Rahab and then report back their findings.

Andrew was to guide them safely to the edge of the city, wait for their return, and guide them safely back to camp.

Andrew's task was dangerous because of the king's soldiers that patrolled that part of the land. They were fierce and mighty soldiers, very large in size, and would give their life to protect the king.

The spies followed their instructions to visit Rahab, who would become a most valuable ally. She would risk her life by telling the king's soldiers the spies had been there but had gone. She hid them on her roof until it was safe for them to leave. In return, they promised to save her and her family when they overtook Jericho. Rahab was to hang the red rope in her window, the one she had used to lower the spies down the wall with. This would be a sign not to touch this home or anyone who lived there.

Andrew waited patiently for the spies to return. Soon after the sun came up on the third day, he heard a noise in the woods. Hiding quietly, he prepared to fight if needed. Suddenly the two spies ran past him, with two of the king's soldiers hot on their heels.

He quickly jumped out, drawing his sword in their defense. The soldiers fought hard, but Andrew was fast and strong and a very skilled warrior. He managed to take one out. He continued to fight for his life with the other soldier. This soldier was much bigger and stronger, with cold eyes that declared Andrew's death. He struck Andrew across the arm with his large sword, and Andrew knew he had been injured badly. He was thrown off balance by the hard blow. He fell to the ground but quickly rolled over and threw up his shield as the soldier raised his mighty weapon to finish the job. Andrew managed to keep his shield up, defending the hard blows. Over and over, the soldier struck him.

Growing weaker, Andrew felt he couldn't hold out much longer. He closed his eyes and told God he was ready to die if it was His will. The enemy warrior suddenly cried out in fear and ran. Andrew looked up from under his shield to see a war angel of the Lord. The angel was bigger than most humans and equipped with a solid gold breastplate. His shield was also gold and trimmed in fine diamonds. He carried a two-edged silver sword that would have cut through ten men. His eyes were focused only on his assigned task. He never spoke but tipped his shield to Andrew as any comrade would and was gone.

Struggling to get up, Andrew found the spies who were hidden in the bushes.

"We are safe now. There will be no more trouble from the king's soldiers," said Andrew.

A few hours later, the three men arrived back at camp. Joshua greeted them and praised their courage. They reported the information on Jericho and told him all about Rahab.

Hannah and Thaddeus came running after hearing the news of Andrew's return.

Thaddeus was upset to see his dad injured. He took his heavy equipment and helped his mother get him home.

Hannah began to bind Andrew's wounds and feed him.

Andrew looked at his beautiful family and gave thanks for them.

"Father, tell me everything. I want to know how you fought off the king's soldiers, how big they were, what size their swords were. Were they ugly, father? Did they have beards? Please, tell me all about your adventure," asked Thaddeus.

"My son, war times are never an adventure. Lives are at stake, and all lives are gifts from our God. I fight in the Lord's army, and I'm proud to do what God asks of me. I have many talents, all gifts from our Father. They are only to be used in obedience to Him. One day, my son, you will recognize your talents. And my prayer is you will use them to honor God. Thaddeus, God's plan for you may not be the same as His plan for me. Perhaps you will never be a soldier. You may have a very different gift. One thing is sure. God will equip you with the right gifts to do what He asks of you. You will have to be the one to decide whether or not to obey," said Andrew.

Thaddeus knew at that moment that he was loved unconditionally. He knew that, no matter what direction he chose, he was loved.

Walking into the kitchen, he saw tears in his mother's eyes. She had overheard their conversation. Looking at Thaddeus with a warm smile, she said, "I love him, too."

Thaddeus picked up his Bible scroll and his beautiful trumpet and went to his special place in the hills. He sat quietly for a while, thinking of the wonderful things God had done for him—his parents, Seth, Joshua, and, soon, the Promised Land.

As he read the scroll, he began singing thanks to his God. He found himself writing songs of praise, accompanied by a melody that would have brought tears to anyone who heard it.

Joshua was also up in the hills praying, as he did every day. He watched young Thaddeus, and knew he was special. Joshua saw that even at a young age, Thaddeus had chosen to give everything to God. He was so touched by Thaddeus's devotion that he stepped out and approached him.

"Oh, Joshua. I didn't know you were here. Forgive me for disturbing you," said Thaddeus.

"No, my boy. It's just the opposite. I think I disturbed you," said Joshua.

They both laughed as they sat together and talked.

Joshua wanted to know how Andrew was doing. He was glad to hear that he was healing.

He began to tell Thaddeus some of the history of his great Levi tribe. It is an honor to be a part of this tribe, you know. Aaron, the first high priest, is a descendent of your great tribe. You know it is the tribe our priest is chosen from.

Thaddeus became fascinated with the priests, their duties, and their abilities to play such beautiful music. He asked Joshua deep and important questions about God and their journey. He was especially interested in how and why the Israelites could so easily lose their faith in such a good and loving God.

Joshua and Thaddeus talked for hours and realized they had very similar feelings, especially about the God they served.

Early the next morning, the trumpets blew, summoning all the tribes to gather as Joshua spoke. Thaddeus and his parents made their way to the meeting place. All the tribes gathered quickly to hear the message. There was talk among the people that it was time to call on the armies to overtake Jericho. Some were saying that Joshua was doing nothing to help them, and they feared for their lives.

Thaddeus knew God was in control and that Joshua would follow the instructions of the Lord.

Joshua began by saying, "I Joshua, son of Nun, tell you God has given Jericho over to us. This is the word of the Lord. These are the instructions God spoke to me. Our soldiers will march around the walls of the town for six days. There will be seven priests that will walk with their trumpets of ram's horns in front of the Ark of the Covenant. On the seventh day, they will march around the city seven times, with the priests blowing the trumpets. When the priests sound a long blast from their trumpets, God has commanded the army to give a loud shout; at that point, the wall will collapse, and the army will go in and take over the city."

Once again Joshua reminded the people that this was the word given to him from the Lord.

People began shouting to Joshua, saying that this was a crazy plan, and it would never work.

"These are God's instructions, and this is what we will do," Joshua told them. "I am asking that we all stop and give God the praise He deserves for giving Jericho over to us. Do not lose faith. This is a time to remember how far God has brought us and that He has never broken a promise to us."

Joshua told the people that he had another important message from God. "In the last month, one of our seven priests had to step down due to illness. God has chosen one of the youngest men our people have ever had. After a long conversation with this talented and wise young man, I give you our next priest, Thaddeus, son of Andrew, from the tribe of Levi," shouted Joshua.

Thaddeus could hardly believe what he had heard. This was the greatest blessing that he could have imagined. Andrew and Hannah beamed with excitement for their son. Seth jumped and shouted with joy for his best friend.

Thaddeus remembered what his father had told him. *God's plan may be very different for you,* and wow, was he right.

There was an anointing of Thaddeus by Joshua and the other priests.

The high priest draped a beautiful cape around him. Thaddeus slowly knelt while Joshua placed his hand on his head, followed by the other six priests also placing their hands on Thaddeus. Joshua prayed a beautiful prayer of thanks and blessings over Thaddeus and presented him to the people.

The priests began to play their trumpets to welcome Thaddeus to this most privilege position.

It was a day that Thaddeus and his parents would always cherish.

The next day would be the start of taking over Jericho, the city that God had promised would be theirs.

Thaddeus didn't sleep much. He was up before the sun, ready to honor and obey God with his beautiful horn trumpet.

"Thaddeus, please eat something. You will need your strength today," said his mother.

"I'm not hungry, mother. I'm much too nervous to eat. Besides, I need to go. Joshua said I should be there before the sun is fully risen," Thaddeus told her.

Andrew and Hannah hugged their son. Andrew prayed for God's will to be done this day.

Thaddeus was off to the greatest honor of his life.

The armies and the priest were all taking their places. Thaddeus's hands were shaking, but he managed to take his trumpet and test blow it a few times. His trumpet gave him a calmness, and he settled in, ready to fulfill God's plan.

Joshua walked around, making sure everyone was in place. He looked over the armies, the special priest that carried the Ark of the Covenant, the seven priests with horns of ram's trumpets, and the guard that followed the Ark of the Covenant.

Everything seemed to be in place, and Joshua gave the command to begin the march.

They marched that day and for the next five days following. On the seventh day, they were up before daybreak to begin their final day. Marching seven times around the city just as instructed, Thaddeus and the other priest sounded the trumpets as loud and long as they could blow. At that moment, Joshua commanded the armies, "Shout to the Lord!"

The great walls of the city fell just as God had promised they would. Only the home of Rahab would be left standing.

Overcome with the greatness of God, Thaddeus bowed and gave thanks.

This would be the beginning of a long journey for Thaddeus. He would be a priest for many years to come and would witness great things that only the one true God could accomplish.

Thaddeus, son of Andrew, would be known for his great wisdom; his devotion to God; his poetry and beautiful music, which continue to touch hearts to this day.

The Innkeeper's Son

It was a beautiful day. Danny and Andrew were playing tag in the open pastures where Andrew lived. His father was a shepherd, and Andrew hoped to follow in his footsteps one day.

Danny's family owned the local inn in Bethlehem. It was the only one in town but never stayed very busy. It only had a few rooms, but they were nice and clean. His dad also had stables where he took care of the animals for their guests. Some came by horse, some by camel, and a few had donkeys. Danny had to help with cleaning the stables. It was not his favorite job.

He had other plans for when he grew up. He dreamed of going to Rome and becoming a doctor. He loved to care for the injured animals or mend the wounds of his brothers when they got hurt.

But for now, he worked with his parents, keeping their inn the best it could be.

His father always taught him that God's Word says that our name is more valuable than gold. "Hard work builds a good name," was his dad's favorite quote.

The boys' lives were somewhat different, but they each had caring parents who taught them the love of God.

The boys were curious about the king that God had promised to send. Surely, he would be a great man with lots of gold and silver.

"I bet he even has a palace," said Andrew.

"Oh yes, with big, golden doors," said Danny.

The Bible scroll was a big part of their lives, and they enjoyed talking about the prophecies of Isaiah.

"Myrtle, my dad's favorite sheep, will be having a baby lamb soon, and he has promised to give me the baby. My dad said it was time that I started my own herd. He said it would be the only lamb he could spare, and if I lost it, I would never have a herd of my own. I'm not worried, because I will be a great shepherd just like my dad," said Andrew.

"Wow, that's fantastic. I can't believe you will have your own herd soon," replied Danny. "Well, I'd better go," he added. "I have to help Father with extra work for the next few days."

"What's going on to keep you so busy?" asked Andrew.

"Do you remember Caesar Augustus's order that a census would be taken to count the people and everyone would have to return to their hometowns to register?" asked Danny. "Many people will have to return to Bethlehem to register. My parents are excited because the inn will stay full for a while, and it will bring in extra money. My parents are going to use the money for my education."

"That's great," said Andrew. "Looks like good things are happing for both of us."

The day was fading fast, and Danny had to run to make it home before dark.

"Danny," called his mother, "hurry and go to the stables and help your father."

Today he did not mind the dirty work in the stables. This time, he would be working to become the doctor that he dreamed about.

The time for the census was getting closer, and Danny decided to go see Andrew one last time before the rush hit.

They met in their usual place under the big tree in the middle of the pasture.

Andrew took Danny to see Myrtle. "It's almost time for her to give birth," said Andrew.

"It's really amazing how God created us and the animals. It's one of the great miracles for sure," said Danny. "I can't wait to learn all about our bodies and how everything works. I want to find cures for illnesses and give help to anyone who needs it."

"You are going to be the best doctor in the world," said Andrew.

The boys headed back to the big tree. They were tired, and this was the best place in Bethlehem to relax.

Their conversation turned to the writings of Isaiah and how there would be a child born who would be their Savior.

"It's said that a pure young woman will give birth. He will be from the house of David," said Danny.

"Hey, that means his family would have to come to Bethlehem to register," said Andrew.

"You're right. They would have to come back here," said Danny, adding, "Well, we won't know for sure when.

108

"I have to go. It's getting late, and I have to finish the stables before dark."

"I'll let you know when my lamb is born," shouted Andrew.

The time came for all to come and register. It was the most crowded Danny had ever seen Bethlehem. The little inn was full and busy. The whole family was working hard to keep up. Danny was responsible for the animals and keeping the stables clean.

The winds began to change as cooler weather started moving in. It felt good to Danny as he worked hard in the stables.

Early the next morning, Andrew came to show Danny his new little lamb. She was soft and fluffy with two brown spots on her back. Andrew was a very proud shepherd. The boys played with the lamb while trying to think of just the right name for her. "I'm thinking of calling her Alpha, because she is the first of my herd," said Andrew proudly.

"That's perfect," said Danny.

"Alpha it is. She will be my pride and joy," replied Andrew.

The boys said their goodbyes as each headed back to finish his work. It was a long day for Danny. The work never stopped, and he was beginning to wish it would hurry and end.

Later that evening before dinner, Danny's mother and father presented him with a gift. He was so excited that he could hardly contain himself. His father said, "This is the extra earnings from the census. It is enough there for the education you want so much."

Danny had never felt so special and excited to hold the only future he'd ever wanted in his hands. *Hard work does pay off,* he thought. *And I will work harder than anyone to become a great doctor.*

They were laughing and enjoying their meal when they heard a tap at the door. His father opened the door to see a humble man and young woman. She was great with child.

"Sir," the stranger said, "we have been to all of my relatives, and none have room left for us. This is our last resort. Could we get a room? As you can see, the baby is due any time now."

Danny's father and mother felt terrible that they had no more rooms. The kind man dropped his head as he smiled and walked away.

"Father, what about the stables?" asked Danny. "I have kept it very clean, and it's warm and out of the weather. I will go make a place for them.

Father made the offer to the man, who graciously accepted.

Danny helped with their donkey and cart. He led them to the nicest and cleanest stable in the barn. He gathered clean sweet hay and brought in water for them.

"How can I ever thank you, Danny?" said the man. "My name is Joseph, and this is Mary."

There was something special about this couple that Danny couldn't explain. He felt as if God was drawing him to help them.

"I will sleep in the other stall and help you if you need me tonight," said Danny.

"Thank you, my boy. You will be a great comfort to us," said Joseph.

This made Danny feel important, and it confirmed his feeling that he was being obedient to God's calling.

It was close to midnight when Danny heard the loud scream of the young woman. "It's time, Danny," called Joseph. "I'll need your help."

Danny collected clean cloths and a pan of water for Joseph. He sat quietly over by the old cow and waited.

It seemed to take forever, but soon he heard the sweet sounds of a child crying. Danny was filled with excitement that he had played a small part in the baby's new life.

Suddenly, Danny saw a bright light glowing over the stables. He ran out to find it was a star in the East. He had never seen anything like it. It was as if the heavens had announced the birth of this baby boy.

This must be the Christ child, God's Son, just as it was told in the Bible scroll, thought Danny.

He ran into the house and grabbed the coins that had been given to him for his education and headed back to the stable.

In the distance, Danny saw Andrew, his father, and the other shepherds coming toward the stable. Danny ran to them with the good news of the Christ child.

Andrew began telling Danny about the angel who had appeared over their field, telling them the good news of the birth of the Messiah. "It was amazing. We were all afraid, but the angel said he was sent by God to tell us the good news that would bring great joy to all people—that today in Bethlehem a child was born. He was the Messiah. Suddenly, a great heavenly host of angels began singing and praising God. Glory to God in highest heaven, and peace on earth to all."

The boys were so excited they had to stop to catch their breath from talking.

"I see you brought Alpha to meet the Christ child," said Danny.

"Well, actually I'm going to give her to the Messiah. Danny, I want to give him the best gift I own, and that's Alpha."

Danny showed Andrew his money bag. "I want to do the same thing. I don't care if I become a doctor or not. Tonight, I want to give all I have to the Christ child."

The boys stopped to thank God for His Son and for providing them with a gift for him.

They humbly took turns kneeling in front of the baby, presenting their gifts. It would be the greatest privilege of their life.

That night the boys realized that with the birth of Jesus, they would be forever changed. "You know, Andrew," said Danny, "my future now is to do what God has planned for me. I am ready to follow him, whether it's to be a stable boy, a doctor, or an innkeeper."

The Bible

Read the story of Noah and how he built a boat.
Learn about Joseph and his rainbow-colored coat,

Jonah in a fish for three days in a row,
All about Jesus. There's so much to know—

Moses on the mountain and the burning bush that
talked,
How the sea would open for their safety as they walked,

Daniel and the lion's den and how God made them
tame,
The healing hand of Jesus for the blind and for the lame.

The little boy's lunch feeding a large crowd in doubt,
The walls of Jericho falling with a mighty shout,

The full armor of God designed with a perfect fit,
Fighting the battles ahead with the strength not to quit.

This wonderful book of truths, breathed from God above,
Is given as guidance for all who accept His love.

Susan Perry